Written By
Derek Smith

ONE FACE

TWO FACE

BLACK FACE

BLUE FACE

D1519070

Illustrated By
Kaede Knipe

WE WISH TO THANK
YOUTUBE CREATOR,
CLYDEDOSOMETHING
FOR HIS ASSISTANCE
WITH CHARACTER
CREATIONS.

THE SOUND OF MY VOICE GIVES NIGHTMARES TO PEOPLE. POLICE HAVE EVEN TOLD ME THAT HONKING IS ILLEGAL!

THE GOVERNMENT NOW USES ME TO MAKE LAWS TO LIMIT YOUR FREEDOMS AND PROMOTE THEIR CAUSE. EVEN CONTENT CREATORS ARE SILENCED AND BANNED FOR CRITICIZING AND SPEAKING OF GOVERNMENT PLANS.

Manufactured by Amazon.ca
Bolton, ON